THE SECRETS OF YOU

A PRACTICAL GUIDE TO USING YOUR HIDDEN POWERS TO ACHIEVE ULTIMATE ABUNDANCE IN ALL AREAS OF YOUR LIFE

ARIF PARMAR

Contents

Acknowledgements

I would like to express my robust gratitude to the many people who saw me through this book; to all those who provided support, talked things over, read, wrote, offered comments, allowed me to quote their remarks, and assisted in the editing, proofreading, and design. I would like to thank all of them, and in particular:

Major Gurpreet Singh and his wife Deepali Singh – mentor, guru, and friend, taught me the basics of telling a story and inspired me to write my first book. If he hadn't encouraged me all the way, I would have given this up a long time ago.

A special thanks to my family who has supported me during the writing of this book even though I was not able to give my full attention to them. Thanks to my friend Kuldipsinh Chavda for his guidance in the creation of my first website and cover page.

Much of what I have learned over the years came as the result of being a son, brother, husband, friend, and enemy may be, though in their ways all this inspired me and, subconsciously contributed a tremendous amount to the content of this book. Thumbs up to all.

Last but not least, a big thanks to Microsoft to develop MS word, we all know how useful the application is! Thanks to Project Gutenberg, which was started in 1971, through this project the grandeur era of eBook takes flight.

CHAPTER ONE

The Secret of the Universe

Let's start with a quick exercise!

I'd like you to force your face into a smile. Go on, don't just sit there actually give it a go! Force your face into a smile, now hold that expression. Everyone knows that when they feel happy, they smile, but the opposite is also true. When you force your face into a smile you start to feel happier. Keep smiling! The same holds for how you talk or even walk, if you put energy into your voice or a spring in your step, you will suddenly feel better. So... you can stop smiling now.

How did it feel??

Did it work for you??

I hope so and next time you want a quick dose of delight just spend 30 seconds or so behaving like a happy person.

What is Universe? I asked and found the answer!!

In my early days and before getting spiritual knowledge from my teacher Major Gurpreet Singh, I have been familiar with the word universe while schooling and on the news/web as 'Miss Universe – Aishwariya Ray'. I am not kidding it's true and maybe you or some of us have meant the universe in this same way, Therefore I have tried out to answer your question (as this same question was to me before I write this book) as enumerated.

I asked and Universe Replies:

I'm not interested in your limiting beliefs;
I'm interested in what makes you limitless.
I'm not interested in your weakness but your strength;
not in your vices but your virtues;
not your insecurities but your greatness.
Stop spinning in your past or on all the reason
you feel you are not good enough.
It's time to step into a higher state
of being above the fray and fear.
It is not what makes you small or limited
that you should be focused on.
It is what makes you magnificent, remarkable,
Loving, blessed...ready.

The universe is always listening to your every thought and every emotion. From the day you came to this planet, the universe has been listening to your every whim and desire, and Guess what, It's Noting it all down in its little notebook. It knows what are the things that will make you happy, and what are the things you dread. it's been there, ever present, ever watching and ever listening to your every word, your every wish, your every desire, and it cares for you so much that every time you make a wish or express a desire, it immediately goes and finds a way to bring your desire to you, and it holds on to it for you until you are ready to receive it (by allowing it).

You are never alone because no matter the circumstances you will always have a friend: 'the universe' and it would make you happy if you wanted to be happy. It will feed you, look after you, take care of you in every possible way... all you have to do is *ASK*...

A Public Service Announcement from The Universe:

I'm no therapist
but I promise you this:
I will listen.
I will care.

Trusting the universe

The universe is a game for anything and everything. It doesn't have any limits, and as a creator, neither do you. Nothing and when I say nothing I mean 'even the most insane most complicated and absurd thing you can imagine is off-limits when it comes to the law of attraction. So next time you encounter a situation you think is difficult or impossible or 'doesn't make sense, think again because I am telling you, it's possible.

It's not always easy to stay feeling positive when what you see isn't what you want. Reading inspirational articles and books helps but what shifts things is when you work from joy within because your subconscious responds to that as the new you. Don't wait to be invited to hang out with friends, throw yourself a dance party- dance by yourself in your room/apartment or on the streets! The endorphin releases your stresses and magically a solution will appear. Trust that you have exactly what you need to create your dreams into reality.

"We often end up paying attention to all the wrong things, be it past, present, or future. Things we don't want, things we want to avoid, worst things, things we wouldn't even want our enemies to go through, but what's the point, we don't realize that by even acknowledging their existence we are inviting them into our experience because the universe listens and delivers without a delay... So, focus responsibly!!.

"Let's face it; our mind is an arrogant fool, who thinks that it knows everything, and whatever it doesn't know, it decides can't be done."

So, it's up to us to not listen to this arrogant fool and decide for ourselves what we are capable of. Often things seem impossible to achieve because the brain doesn't have enough logical information to achieve that particular thing. This is where the knowledge of the universe gives us an upper hand; we can think beyond and around 'what is and go to the place of 'having' our desire even though it isn't there now because, with the power of the universe coupled with the power of our mind, we can achieve even the most distant our dreams.

"There will always be external events and people in your life who will tell you what you can do and what you can't do. But the truth is that your capabilities and your limits are only limited by your mind. When we focus on a task that previously seemed Impossible and play with the possibility of its achievement, the universe responds by showing us the way."

"There will always be external events and people in your life who will tell you what you can do and what you can't do. But the truth is that your capabilities and your limits are only limited by your mind. When we focus on a task that previously seemed Impossible and play with the possibility of its achievement, the universe responds by showing us the way."

Ask-Believe-Receive

Every time we place a request with the universe, it is granted instantly, it's done!! The universe lines up all the coincidences and serendipities to make it happen. The only thing that keeps it away is our negative beliefs. So, if we can only 'Believe' that the universe is actively trying to fulfill our request, it will come to us.

"Believe that it's yours, already, and feel the way you would feel if you already have it.

The universe is listening and responding to our vibration/emotion every second and is responding to it accordingly. So, to make a Shift in our current situation all we have to do is, shift our vibration to match the vibration of what we want and hold on to it. That's all there is to do.

CHAPTER TWO

The Secrets of Law of Attraction

The Universe is not punishing you or blessing you. The universe is responding to the vibrational attitude that you are emitting. - Abraham Hicks

Law of Attraction – Knowledge of LOA.

One fine day, we wake up, watch a great movie like 'The Secret," or read the book and go, "Whoa, I have a magic lamp now; all I got to do is to feel right." It all sounds so easy. We decide that life is our creation, that we are writing our own story, and that we can make anything happen just by thinking the right thoughts and feeling the right feelings and there's nothing wrong with this knowledge, this is pretty much the gist of it all.

Then we start slowly; we dip our toes in the water and start by attracting a cup of coffee or a rainbow (or a picture of it), and again go crazy happy for the power we have freshly discovered that we have. So far, so good. It gets more and more clear that the life we have lived so far was our creation and all that is yet to come is going to be our creation as well. We are amazed by this power that we have.

Slowly and steadily our faith is reaffirmed, and so are our fears.

With the knowledge, that our 'thoughts become things, we begin to monitor our thoughts. Plus, with the knowledge that our feelings act as a fuel that launches those thoughts into the universe, we begin to monitor our feelings as well, and doing that, at some point, we become really scared of our thoughts and feelings.

You see, man is a creature of habits, and old habits die hard. Through no fault of our own, or anyone else for that matter, we have been trained to think through the worst possible scenarios regarding every area of life. Probably our survival instinct has developed our brains this way. However, whatever the case, it's a fact that we cannot change the way we think and feel overnight. Sure, we can start taking baby steps toward great change but doing that overnight poses some serious risks.

Most of us do make this mistake. We decide to make the maximum of the LOA (Law of attraction), but we forget that it's a universe based on thoughts and feelings and those patterns are very slow to change. They require a lot of patience if not hard work.

Most of us get overwhelmed by all the negativity inside us and some of us decide to take the easy and short route. So instead of dealing with the negative emotions inside us and slowly changing those patterns, we start to bottle them up. We ban all kinds of negative thoughts, we stop talking about what is bothering us, and we start pretending that all is well.

We think that if we bottle them up, seal them and then forget about them, they will disappear. They don't and while we get busy with, pretend games, those bottled-up emotions at the back of our minds become ticking time-bomb, ready to explode any minute. Besides, when they do, they leave us perplexed and exasperated like never before. Plus, we feel at loss, as to where to start picking up pieces, and what is the point of it all.

Now, don't go into panic mode, just yet. That is not the objective of this book. The objective is to give you a heads up and possibly prevent you from making a mistake that many of us, (including myself) have made. This will save you one step and a lot of mess and pain.

Do not suppress your emotions. That's all.

Suppressing them won't help. Dealing with them and then letting them go healthily will. If you feel you have been hurt in the past, it's very legitimate to feel the anger inside you. Let it show. Talk to someone you trust about it. Cry, if that feels good. Seek help and you don't even have done this for a long time. You'll start feeling better before you know it. There will be no pretense in that 'good feeling'.

Again, there are no set rules for what you need to do to deal with suppressed emotions. For that, you will need the guidance of your inner self, but one thing

that helps to bring out that inner guidance is meditation. So do meditate and try not to bottle things up inside you. They'll do more harm than good.

The Simplicity of Law of Attraction!

FEELING = RECEIVING

MORE FEELINGS = FASTER RECEIVING

POSITIVE FEELINGS = POSITIVE RECEIVING

NEGATIVE FEELINGS = NEGATIVE RECEIVING

MORE NEGATIVE FEELINGS = WORST SITUATION

MORE POSITIVE FEELINGS = BETTER THE SITUATION

It's so simple if you think about it, the limitation, the whys, the if's, the but's, the how's, and the why me!! 's. All are feelings! Negative feelings!! When we vibrate on these feelings, the universe just listens to us and gives us more circumstances to make us feel more if's and but's and the classic "WHY ALWAYS ME GOD???!!" moments. Well, it's always you, because you always give the wrong signals to the universe. Don't blame God, your ex or your boss, your parents, money, government, or corruption. If anyone is to be blamed for your bad experiences, it's you!! It's all you!! But don't you see now, it's all so logical; it has all been under your control all this time.

Now don't feel bad... everyone screws up, but that's how you GROW!! Now with this knowledge, just forgive yourself.

The process to forgive yourself (Do it before bed)

"Close your eyes, feel your breath and now imagine a door, open it, and there you will see a person, a scared person, that person is you. Ask him/her what's wrong, and where he or thinks has he screwed up. Now one by one take all his screw-ups and tell him that they were just a result of his screwed-up vibration. Tell him it's OK, no need to beat himself up because he didn't know how the universe worked. Tell him that you are there to tell him how the universe works, comfort him, and empower him with your knowledge of the universe and the law of attraction. Talk to him as long as you need, in your mind, or out loud. (i feel a lot better doing it out loud, it's like 2 people talking, except it's just you) convince him, raise him from fear and guilt and tell him it's ok and you have forgiven him and by extension yourself, now hand in hand both of you walk out of that door and Take 3 deep breaths and release!!!"

The process to forgive others (To be done only once)

Sometimes we do feel an urge, to high-five some people, in the face, with a chair!! It's quite natural, even with the knowledge that we now possess as LOAers, that it's not their fault, it's all our screwed-up vibration that caused them to act as they acted but we still want to punish them, and here is a fun way how.

Sit down, close your eyes... now imagine yourself in a theater, not a movie theater, but one where they perform PLAYS and stuff. There is a stage, and on that stage, there is a chair, the person you want to punish is tied to the chair, now begins the fun part, they are at your mercy, Don't hold back, yell at them, they are there to listen, and repent, tell them how they have wronged you, remind them off all the times they have made you feel bad.

Now pass out a sentence, befitting their crimes against you. Imagine them suffering and going through all the punishment, you want them to go through, you can accompany verbal abuse along with it, have fun with it, let your wild side go... um... Wild!! Take all your anger out!! Let it out, until there is no more left inside of you.

Now... after you have made them suffer enough, they will plead for mercy and they will apologize, listen to them until you find an apology that you fully can accept..., Now accept their apology and forgive them. Take 3 deep breaths and release the anger!!

PS. don't do this exercise very often, once for one person is sufficient, so make sure you vent out all your anger.

So, do you see the simplicity??

Feel good = GOOD, Feel Bad = BAD!

It's all in your emotions; all you need to do is be aware of them.

P.S (Bonus) - As you are about to drift to sleep tonight just ask the universe for the following!

"Dear universe/God, I 'want' to feel the way as if my (biggest desire) has come true. "

I think what will follow will be an incredibly high feeling vibration.

What do you want?

What you want is the right question. That is the question you should ask yourselves, and that is the only question you should figure out the answer to. Because once you have figured it out, and decided what you want, the universe starts acting on it. The universe figures the 'How' part of it, the part that you may or may not know, but the universe always knows the best 'How' to get you to your desired 'what'. For your reference given enumerated examples, you can choose. Or you may have your wish list.

-Spirituality

1. To have some clarity of mind;
2. To feel each day nearer to my inner self, be centered;
3. To know me;
4. To have a greater level of spiritual joy that raises me above our human burdens;
5. To live with intention and purpose;
6. To be in the ocean of love and wisdom;

7. To get a meaningful glimpse of the spiritual good side of everyone I come in contact with;

8. To learn how to meditate when you do not have a lot of time to do so;

9. To know how to abandon the shallower world around us to reach greater levels of peace;

10. To feel alive. I know that feeling. It doesn't matter if you feel sad or happy there is a richness to it that is sometimes missing, and I feel a dullness;

11. To feel connected and not separated and lost would change my life;

12. To stop searching for answers to unanswerable questions and just live;

-Meaningful life

13. In the end, to be able to say I made a positive change that had a major effect on a large community (leaving the world better off somehow)

14. To know that I am on the path to finding and following my calling;

15. To help people heal old wounds;

16. To live with intention and purpose;

17. To live my life as I do and want, to grow my soul through the lessons;

18. To be creative;

19. To learn how to stop me from being short with my loved ones when they try to be kind;

20. To understand life's purpose;

21. It would drastically change my life by having a clear objective and a clear way of pursuing it;

-Happiness

22. To be who I am, total connection with my spirit.

23. To end disconnection from others (which leads to loneliness);

24. To be in touch with life;

25. To be intimate and less afraid;

-Peace of mind

26. To have peace of mind and clarity;

27. To be free from worry and fear

28. To honor our bodies, our minds, our spirits – and each other;

29. To feel serenity in making life decisions that are aligned with all those values;

30. To be peaceful so I may be free of these knee-jerk responses so that I may act from compassion and wisdom;

31. To stop my perfectionism and do better at work and in everything else;

32. To have silence in my head;

33. To turn off that inner voice always talking;

34. To get rid of unwanted negative thoughts;

35. To stop judging my thoughts;

36. To ride peacefully with whatever is presented on my journey;

37. To learn how to maintain internal emotional peace (especially from fear), so that I can gain self-confidence.

38. To learn step-by-step processes on how to let go, detach, not judge, and feel inner peace;

39. How to control anguish, and frustration, and not let others harm you;

40. Not to compare my needs with others and be attached to outcomes to look good;

41. How to feel free. I know it is all in my head, but I often feel hindered by other people and their demands. Why can I not be who I am and not feel guilty about it?

-Productivity

42. To master time management;

43. To develop self-discipline;

44. To create good habits;

45. To experience a paradigm shift that helps me view challenges differently, especially relating to self-discipline and motivation;

46. To learn how to be in the zone;

47. To be more productive and focused;

-Self-acceptance and confidence

48. To learn step-by-step processes on how to let go, detach, not judge, and feel inner peace;

49. To quiet the negative self-talk;

50. To move away from negative self-limiting thoughts;

51. To quell my self-doubts and just get on with it so that my life doesn't feel like it's one step forward and two steps back;

52. To recognize all the good in my life, and be content with it.

53. To worry less about my performance at work (which is very high, but due to family conditioning, I always feel 'on trial');

54. To feel more courage, and less embarrassment;

55. To be confident about consistently making good decisions;

-Meaningful work

56. To find a way to earn a living doing something that contributes to others, yet doesn't rob my soul;

57. To find a passion and stick with it;

58. To find a way to pursue my calling while also supporting my family financially.

59. To be able to find fulfillment in my career.

60. To find out how to reconcile productivity and relaxation. Oftentimes I get so engaged in my work that I end up burning out or running into hours for relaxation.

61. To truly zero in on the essence of what my talent or gift is;

62. To realize that what I have to offer is exactly what the world needs at this point;

63. To achieve my fullest potential in terms of skills that I have;

64. To translate my potential into a comfortable lifestyle for me and my family;

65. To feel like I'm not just 'going through the motions at work and remove the feeling that my 'real' life is lived outside of work

66. To know what I want and have the resolve not to re-evaluate it too soon;

-Happiness

67. To feel freer, and that my many, many obligations would not be an obstacle to feel free.

68. To know that what I'm doing is worthwhile – raising a kid, the work I do, the way I live my life and interact with people.

69. To make a positive difference for people close to me and therefore be happy.

70. To maintain a good work/life balance;

So, what do you want today?? Is your business.

Having faith is your action.

"How to get it done??" Is the universe's business...

So just relax and expect a miracle!!

One "Simple Technique" to clear your resistance to stuck desire

When we say "let go of things" we are not even by a long shot referring to your desires, we are referring to the 'things' that are keeping your desire away from you, and to let those things go, we have a small exercise for you.

Find a comfortable place where you can't be disturbed for a while and, close your eyes. Now take a few deep breaths, and concentrate on the cool air going in your nose and the warm air coming out, this will help to clear your mind of any thoughts. You are ready now.

"I want you to imagine a beautiful garden, just be in that garden for a while, notice the flowers the warmth of the sun, and the butterflies. In the middle of the garden, there is a cottage approach the cottage and open the door inside its dark, but you see a child... you look closer, the child is you when you were 5 years old. You notice that the child is scared. You gently approach the child and gently comfort him and ask him what is wrong, and what is he/she afraid of. (Now in this conversation you can talk to the child on the subject of a desire that's been keeping away from you for a while, a desire that's proving a little hard to achieve). The child will tell you all the things that have hurt him regarding the desire, all the things he fears, and of the reasons why the desire can't be achieved. Now being the self-aware and knowledgeable 'LOAer' you know that tackling all these fears and reasons is no big deal for the universe. Your job is to comfort and let the child know this. Convince him, that he no longer needs to fear his fears because the universe is looking out for him and that his desire will be fulfilled as soon as he leaves this darkness and steps out into the garden to enjoy it.

"ALL THAT MATTERS IS HOW YOU VIBRATE IN THE PRESENT MOMENT, WHAT HAPPENED IN THE PAST WAS JUST A RESULT OF YOUR BAD VIBRATION, BUT NOW YOU KNOW BETTER. SO JUST LET GO OF ANGER, FEAR, GUILT, DOUBT AND VIBRATE AS IF YOU WOULD VIBRATE WHEN YOU WILL HAVE YOUR

DESIRE.”

“Make him understand this, talk to him, comfort him, give him a hug, answer all his doubts with your wisdom of the universe, and then when he begins to feel better about the "off-limit desire", walk him out of the cottage and enjoy the sights.

Once you start feeling better on the topic that you have been feeling stuck with for so long, the process is done, take a few deep breaths and open your eyes.

I would recommend you do this exercise right before you go to sleep.

Happy cleansing!!

Revive any relationship with the Law of Attraction!

One of the most common questions that I encounter is, "Can I use the law of attraction to bring back an Ex?"

The answer to this is yes! You can! It’s easy and difficult at the same time but in the end, it will depend on you. It doesn’t matter if the relationship ended yesterday or last month or last year, it doesn’t matter if you are here, and they are 1000 miles away. None of it matters, all that matters is if you still love them.?

Most of you will say, "Yes we do!" That’s why we are here! We have tried for so long now; we have tried every move in some proverbial book! Now we are frustrated, and we have turned to the universe for help. Well, you have come to the right place, but before we start, I want to just make sure that you are pursuing whomever it is you are pursuing because of love, and not to prove a point, not because you think that you can’t get anyone else, not out of fear, not to feed your ego, but because you are in love.

Now how will you know if you are still in love, there are a million ways to know, but asking yourself and talking to yourself works best.

PROCESS TO DETERMINE IF YOU STILL LOVE THEM!

1. Find a quiet place where no one can disturb you for at least 15 minutes.

2. Now sit down in a comfortable position and close your eyes.

3. Take a few deep breaths.

4. Now just for a moment, concentrate on yourself, be entirely present at the moment, pay attention to your body, and how it feels, just pull out all your awareness from the past, and future, and be there in your body, be with yourself.

5. Know that at this moment, sitting right here right now, you are free from everything. There is nothing that you need to do, there is nowhere that you need to be and there is nothing that can hurt you. For these, 15 minutes you are here, and you are free from all the worldly affairs of your life. These 15 minutes are yours to relax! So, relax!

6. Now when you feel like it, search your awareness, and find the most amazing person aside from your ex that you know. This person can be anyone; someone you once had a crush on, someone who is way better than your ex in looks, nature, and all other aspects.

7. Once you have zeroed in on that better person. Ponder this question. "Would I still want my ex if this amazing person walked up to me and proposed to me?"

8. For a Moment consider this, believe it is true, if this amazing person that you know of, or someone like that comes up to you tomorrow and proposes to you, would you go for them or would you still want to patch things with

your ex.

Take a moment to process this thought in detail.

If you happily accepted this new and amazing person, then I must tell you that, you are not in love with your ex. What you are looking for is a happy and loving relationship, and that can come from anyone, it doesn't have to be your ex.

Now if the thought of accepting this new and improved person gave you mixed feelings, like cheating on your ex, even though you are not in a relationship as of now, or if the thought of losing your ex (despite all the kinks) popped up, and it didn't feel good. Then yes, you are still in love with your ex, and you should move on.

When you get to know someone, all their physical characteristics start to disappear. You being to dwell their energy, recognize the scent of their skin. You see only the essence of the person, not the shell. That's why you can't fall in love with beauty or looks. You can lust after it, be infatuated by it, and want to own it. You can love it with your eyes and your body, not your heart. That's why when you connect with a person, physical imperfections disappear and become irrelevant.

Moving On...

Now the first thing to know is that it is possible! It is easy! It is already done! All you have to do is relax and let the manifestation in. (What is the manifestation?#? You will read about this in Chapter #3)

Relaxing ain't that easy in these situations, there is so much pain and hurt feelings and memories, that you are in a constant battle with yourself. So first we have to take care of these feelings. You must know that these feelings of fear and insecurity are the ones that landed you here in this situation in the first place.

The universe always monitors how you feel and then tries to mold your experience accordingly so that you can have more of those feelings.

YOUR FEELING IS THE ONLY THING THAT MATTERS.

Certain things generally cause relationships to go bad. I'll try to list all of them and discuss how to tackle them.

Feeling of unworthiness

So, you met the guy/girl of your dreams, someone whom you would have never thought you can get in your wildest dreams. You got lucky. You put them on a pedestal, and all of creation and god's creatures including you come in second place to your guy/girl. You are willing to change for them. You are so much in love that you get the stars and the moon for them, and you are perfectly happy with the 50-Rs card they bought for you on your special day. You eat what they eat, you go where they go.

This is where things go bad. Sometimes while doing these things, you start to lose yourself, when you think that your lover is out of your league, or superior to you, it gives out a signal of unworthiness to the universe. Plus, the universe responds to it, by increasing your lover's value in your eyes and decreasing your value in your eyes. So, when a problem arises, even a small one you give up rationality and start looking for what 'you' did wrong. With time the universe gives you more and more circumstances that make you feel more and more worthless.

"So, what can I do about it??"

Love yourself, value yourself. You should know that we live in a vibrational universe and in the eyes of the universe everyone is equal, everyone is beautiful, and everyone is capable of greatness. When you first met the love of your life, it was you and your vibration that attracted them. The universe doesn't decide your worth. You DO! It is your belief that drives the universe to bring things into your experience. If you believe you are worthy, then you are worthy. There is nothing wrong with you. You deserve to be put on a pedestal, you deserve to be loved and valued the same way you love and value your lover and they will be happy to move the heavens and earth for you because they love you. When you truly believe this, the universe will start to change your experience.

A Simple Technique to Become Closer to a Person (Ex/ New) Using LOA!!

First order of business... clear your resistance regarding the situation with that person, because depending on your relationship history with the individual in question, there can be a lot of hurt feelings, anger, guilt, resentment blah blah, etc etcetera. As explained in Chapter #2 you have tried the technique to clear your stuck desire.

Now once you have gotten rid of your resistance, and you are feeling better and much more hopeful, follow these steps.

1. Sit down and relax, take a few deep breaths, and feel the cool air entering your nose and the warm air going out. Concentrate on your breathing, this will help you clear your mind and help you focus.

(Now before you proceed I want you to remember, that the moment you start feeling better, the universe starts to work for you, it's your first manifestation, which means the universe has started on your manifestation.)

2. Now I want you to take your time and think about any good times you had with this person, I want you to one by one pull up all the fondest memories you have with this person and make a list of them, just describe each memory in a line and also try to live them again and, not in detail but just to remember how you felt that time.

3. Now from this list of the fondest memories, choose your favorite one. Describe it as if it were a chapter from the book "The incredible life of (enter your name)". Take a pen and paper and describe the whole thing down, the more the details, the more fun it would be. Just try to have fun with this and try to relive that amazing moment.

4. If I am any good as an instructor, you should be feeling a lot better about this particular person by now. This good feeling for that person indicates that the universe has accepted your quest to bring this person into your life and is on its way to making things happen.

5. Now, take a moment to accept the fact that by doing this exercise and by feeling good about this person you are inviting him/her into your life, to make more memories like the ones you just described, and that the good feeling was a sign from the universe that the universe is on your case.

6. Create an anchor of this memory, by describing it on a piece of paper, or if you have a pic for that memory even better, put it up somewhere you can see it 10 times daily. The more the better!! The idea is to make that memory an anchor, which is going to send you back to the good times and invoke that good feeling every time you see it.

So, if you are still holding on to or hiding any kind of frustration or resentment within you, find the nearest garbage bin and throw it away because the universe is on your manifestation, you just manifested that person, by feeling good, and now it's just a matter of time, just let the universe do its job, for god's sake, do not interfere with the universes working by pursuing this person yourself. Let the universe deliver them to you.

Tips to get back with your exes.

When an ex blocks you suddenly (i.e., on Facebook) negativity becomes your best friend- you go into panic mode, your heart starts pounding, your head starts swirling and you sink into an ugly depression. You feel rejected, unloved, and unwanted.

For nothing.

Switch your thoughts to something more positive because let me tell you- there are 2 reasons why an ex would block you:

1. They are hurting. People block their exes because they couldn't stomach seeing pictures of them- every time they see them, invokes feelings of love from their higher selves, and their lower self who is not in sync starts to feel bad.

2. To provoke a reaction out of you.

Now, if you ignore the temporary bump and continue focusing on YOU and what you want and not them- with time the universe will provide you what you want i.e.; a happy relationship back with them or something even better, if you are vibing at the place of "Them or something better" and they will get in touch with you be it 3 weeks or 3 months.

Please don't panic. Everything is in divine timing. People (especially exes) only have the power to upset and hurt you if you allow it. CHOOSE to be happy.

"This situation of attracting back an ex is two-sided, You are either focused upon their absence, telling the universe that you want them because they are not there, asking yourself, why it went wrong, and what's wrong with you, wondering on what ifs, if this is the case, then let me tell you that things are going to get worse for you, and you are going to end up losing them.

OR

If you can bring yourself to a place where their absence doesn't matter to you or their absence doesn't bother you, you are anymore and from that place of calmness and peace if you can anticipate their arrival in the best possible way. Then they will be back before you know it! "

Hope this helps!!

CHAPTER THREE

The Secret of Manifestation

Thought is Energy, to create it (energy), Just use your imagination. - Albert Einstein

The Law of Manifestation

This quote is more accurate than perhaps Einstein realized. Creative visualization is the easiest way to be a creation of manifestation but just having a daydream is not enough.

The law of manifestation is also known as the Law of Beamed Energy. The divine is governed by a series of laws that brings order and balance to the natural universe. Without Chaos, there cannot be ordered. Without order, there cannot be Chaos. Therefore, there cannot be balance. One day we'll get into why this is important.

The Law of Manifestation defines or explains; however, you want to perceive it, how we as humans, create that which we want. The key to this law is that we create what we want and not necessarily what we need. So, the adage, be careful what you ask for - you might get it, is very true. It's easy to create, but not necessarily easy to deal with what you've created.

It's also easy to create material things. Much harder to create emotional things, especially those that include someone else. Such as relationships, fertility, and even revenge.

So, what is the Law of Manifestation?

Thought is the creator behind all operations of manifestations in the material world. These manifestations cannot occur until a suggestion or thought, (some would call it a desire) hits the subconscious mind but the subconscious must also 'take in' that thought and process it.

Visualization has its process of creation. Simply put, Visualization is the act of deliberately bringing into manifestation a desire or need by an exercise of picturing that object in the 'mind's eye (one key point), as if the object is already in your possession (the second key point). This process, when performed successfully, will eventually become a thought form that is strong enough to manifest in the outer world, or physical world.

Manifesting vision

After a meditation, visualize what you want. Imagine it in as much detail as possible. Speak to it, and put all the effort you can into that one creative desire. You can do this in a couple of ways. One easy method is to imagine and feel the vision going from your creative mind into your 3rd eye (the point between your eyes and above the brow). Give it form and energy from your desire.

Now, this method requires you to record what you want in your journal, grimoire, or book of shadows. Before you begin, record what you want, and what you're planning to do. Document all the detail needed for your visualization after the meditation. After your chosen method of manifestation, record what you did, what you felt and anything extra you want to keep in writing. When your desire does manifest, record how it came to you, and now that you have it, what shall occur, and don't forget a 'Thank you to the universe for the assistance in the manifestation.

Manifestation Process

I learned about the process of manifestation which says our...

Thoughts –> Feelings –> Actions –> Results

I think this definition of the process of manifestation is mostly true, but I like to add beliefs to the mix. It's my experience that our thoughts come from our deepest beliefs which live in our subconscious minds. So, if we put beliefs before thoughts, we get this...

Beliefs –> Thoughts –> Feelings –> Actions –> Results

If you've lived for a very long, it's easy to see that our beliefs become reinforced by our life experiences. If you touch a hot stove as a child, your mind (and body) is quickly taught the belief that "stoves can cause pain". This creates a belief (neuro associative memory) deep in your subconscious mind that causes you to think again before you touch a hot stove.

The not-so-good news is that we also pick up limiting or non-supportive beliefs as we grow up, too. As kids, we're exposed to so many experiences and with every experience, we make up stories or choose beliefs, some empowering and some that hold us back from our potential.

Instant Manifestations!!

Yes, that's a thing. All manifestations are instant. The universe listens to your intention and immediately rushes to gather all the cooperative components that will help you get what you want. Unless you don't stand in its way.

Some of you will agree, and some of you will not, some will say that for 'small' things it's possible, but 'Big' things always take time. I say no, it's all relative, let's take an example,

Example: You are sitting at home and suddenly you find yourself craving your favorite food, so you just thought about it and felt the taste in your mouth and made a mental note that you are going to have it ASAP (as soon as possible), then you drift off to other things completely forgetting about the food. That night at dinner you discover that your mom or your spouse/mom has made your favorite food for you, or you find yourself dining at the place that serves your favorite food and Manifestation! (And you didn't have to make any effort, no imagination, or visualization, nothing, it was just your love for that particular thing, and the feeling of it being an achievable goal that manifested it.)

Now think of a homeless guy, who hasn't had anything to eat in a week, what do you think happens when he thinks about his favorite food?? He immediately is smacked in the face with the thought that he can't afford it, dammit he can't even afford regular food, and the favorite food would be a miracle! It's a big thing for him, this thought of enjoying his favorite delicacy is a 'big' thing for him, whereas it's a 'small' thing for you.

So, you see the point there is no such thing as "BIG" or "SMALL" because the standard of BIG or SMALL can't be different for different people. It's all in your vibration. It's all the same for the universe. If you can cut through the crap, that's telling you that something is BIG for you, then you can have an INSTANT MANIFESTATION!

It's all about raising your vibration to a place where your desire doesn't look like a BIG thing.

"NOW HOW DO I DO THAT? You ask"

Well, BY RAISING YOUR VIBRATION! by being Happy!

These will help.

1. Exercise.
2. Spend time with nature.
3. UP your Oxygen Intake.
4. Keep trying for small manifestations and keep upping the stakes. i.e., first a chocolate, then coffee, then catching up with an old friend, Manifest a call from someone distant. So on and so forth. This will increase your trust in the universe.

Process for Instant Manifestations

"Sit down, relax, close your eyes if you like, now take 3 deep breaths, with every exhale, feel yourself calming down and relaxed, take more deep breaths until you are fully relaxed, there you are at a high vibration now. Now, think about the thing you want, if it's chocolate, then feel the taste in your mouth, if it's a person, then feel the taste in your mouth I'm kidding!!, Just think about how much you like having that person around, feel the love the happiness, the fun, if it's something else then feel the feeling of having it, like if receiving some extra cash will give you relief, Then feel relieved. Now hold that feeling for as long as you want. Enjoy it. Now when you are ready, let go. It will come to you in the next 48 hours but if you don't go on checking every 5 minutes. Checking on a manifestation will send a signal of doubt. Just forget about it.

Go on try it.

A Quick Manifestation Drill!

This quick and easy exercise is for those times when you are feeling particularly enthusiastic and want to create something just for the fun of it. This is also for the newbies who wish to experiment and make sure that this stuff works. You can also use this to let go of something you wish would come to you. Here's the drill, and it's fun too, so enjoy

1. Find a quiet place where you won't be disturbed for 15-20 minutes.

2. Sit down comfortably, (you can also lie down), close your eyes, and start taking deep but gentle breaths.

3. Keep your gentle focus on your breathing until your mind starts to calm.

4. Now, with your eyes closed, imagine yourself sitting in the garden, and trying to feel the details of your favorite garden; freshness in the air, the warmth of sunshine on your face.

5. Imagine that there is a big bubble of pink color floating just above your head. Whatever wish you would put in this bubble will come true.

6. Now as your eyes are still closed, imagine your desire. Make the image as vivid as possible; imagine every little detail, the feel of its touch, its smell, and most importantly, the happiness inside you that this desire of yours will give you.

7. After its starts to feel real, put the object of your desire in the pink bubble that's floating just above your head. Trust that as soon as you put it there, your order with

the universe is placed.

Imagine that pink bubble float away up in the sky. Keep tracking it till it's no longer visible.

Universe has now started working on your desire, feel the gratitude, as your wishes are being granted very soon.

You can now open your eyes and do whatever is the most fun for you.

CHAPTER FOUR

The Secret of Vibration

A way out of negativity!

So, what's the deal with the universe anyway??? From what we have been hearing, the universe responds to your vibration... good or bad vibration is responded with matching manifestations. The universe is neutral when it comes to manifestations, and you are the one responsible for your vibrations and your manifestations.

So be afraid, be very afraid... because there is no one coming to your rescue, it's all your responsibility.

This one thought drives a lot of new LOAers up the walls. You start reveling in the awesome power of the universe, and then you have a negative thought, and you get scared, because negative thoughts attract to you more negative thoughts, and in turn negative situations and manifestations, so you try to wrestle that negative thought to the ground, and in doing so, you make the situations even worst.

Ok, have I scared you enough?? I have!? I am sorry...

Ok, let me put this one scary thought to ease...

The universe is inherently good. The universe is actively trying to take us to our desires. The universe knows what makes you happy and what are your inner and deepest desires, and it always is actively trying to push you towards your happiness, but we hold ourselves in a place of misery by actively holding on to the negative thoughts.

Do you know why the negative feelings or emotions cause so much pain?? Because you are like that lighthouse that is standing against the huge waves. The waves (the universe) are constantly trying to sway you and sweep you towards your happiness, but you are being stubborn, and you are standing in negativity (like the lighthouse). The pain that you feel is caused because by holding yourself in a place of negativity (worrying, acknowledging absence, anger, betrayal); you are constantly waging a war against the universe that is trying to take you to your happiness.

So, don't you think that giving up is the right thing to do? When you surrender yourself to the universe, it takes you to the place where all your desires and manifestations are waiting for you. All you have to do is let go and give in.

When we feel stuck or when we are in a bad place, that only means we have created too much negative momentum i.e., we are stuck in a web of negativity, and the more we try to find our way out of it, the tighter its grip on us becomes.

So, when we give in, when we let go, we try to go to a place of calm and comfort, where this tangled web of negativity slowly starts to get loose, and the more 'still' we become, the further out of this web we find ourselves. Until there comes a point where there are no more negativities left, and from here the universe swoops in like superman... and carries us to our goals.

The flow of the Universe

>>>>>>>>>>>>>> Your Desires.

<<<<<<<<<<<<<< Direction our negativity is dragging us towards.

You may visualize, imagine, appreciate, and if it's working, good for you, but for those, who feel that all this feels a bit forced. Know that you can't go from a place of negativity to a place of positivity directly. You have to go to a place of calmness before. The best way to stop negative thoughts is to stop thoughts altogether.

Bad feelings Calmness/Content Happiness

>>

So, how do you come to a place of calmness? How do you stop the thoughts???

You meditate!!

The universe is always listening and responding to our emotional state/ vibration. So, what you have been experiencing and whatever you are going to experience is all dependent on how you feel/vibrate.

The BIG REVEAL - It's a choice! EVEN BIGGER - IT'S YOUR F#&KING CHOICE. You are the one in control. "For god's sake just disregard everything and feel good already!!"

The Formula to a Happy Life

"The meaning of life is not to live forever, something that will"
– Deepali Singh

Let go!! Make peace with the past, it's a story that you can share with others if it's inspiring and good or learns from if it's bad and full of mistakes. The biggest lesson to be learned from the past is that "WE LIVE IN A VIBRATIONAL WORLD". We give out vibration and the universe responds to our vibration, that is how our experience on this plane is created.

Whatever we have experienced till now, was a result of our negative vibration (fear, guilt, insecurity, rage, uncertainty, anxiety, self-loathing, low self-esteem), so acknowledge it and let it go, just sit down, and look at how much destruction these negative feelings have caused in your life already, and if we hold on to them, then our future will be destroyed.

NOW is the place, where your power lies, it is NOW when you will go to the mirror and talk yourself out of these negative vibrations/feelings and convince yourself to create an amazing future, by vibrating positively.

Patience is a good thing, but it's not necessary.

"When you understand the Law of Attraction, and when you begin to deliberately direct your thoughts, the things you desire will flow quickly and steadily into your experience - and patience will not be necessary."

"We are not excited about anyone learning patience, for it implies that things naturally take a long time, and that is not true. They only take a long time in coming when your thoughts are contradicted. If you move forward then backward and then forward then backward, you could potentially never get to where you want to go. But when you stop moving backward and only move forward, you will get there quickly and that does not require patience." – Abraham Lincoln

It's all about our Vibration/Emotion.

The universe is picking up on your vibration 24x7. That is its only job, and your only job is to be aware of your vibration and diligently work on keeping your vibration up. Every moment of your life till now has played out last because of the vibrations you offered before or during that moment. Your achievements, as well as your failures (i like to call them lessons), are there as a result of your vibration. So where are you vibrating today??

Levitating your vibs

Raising your vibration is the best way to get the universe to do your bidding. Whenever you start to feel a better feeling emotion it indicates a rise in your vibrational state, and the universe quickly responds to it, by helping you raise your vibration even more, and then you just don't stop. I have found a few ways that help me raise my vibration.

1. Physical exercise/Yoga
2. Meditation.
3. Practicing appreciation/Gratitude.

"Realize deeply, that the 'Present moment i.e., Now' is all that you have. Life in itself is a collection of millions of 'NOW' moments. So then why wait, gather your thoughts wherever they may be, and focus on the 'Now'?

Be happy 'NOW'

Be aware of the 'NOW'.

Your power is 'NOW'.

If not now, When?

CHAPTER FIVE

The Secret of You

Know your worthiness

So here you are, intelligent, funny, hardworking, and playing by the rules, but you have had a string of bad relationships, that member of the opposite sex, that you always notice, doesn't notice you instead he/she is into some jerk!

Here you are, hardworking, and more intelligent and competent than the rest of the idiots at your office, but still, you are stuck in a crappy routine job surrounded by idiots, and clearly, they don't pay you enough to put up with kind of work that they take from you.

So, why is this? Why is it that you from time to time cross paths with someone whom you know is a 'jerk' yet has everything you ever wanted?

The answer is simple, it's belief! They believe that "They are worthy" and that bring to them whatever they desire.

You and I and everyone we know live in a vibrational world, i.e., everything we see and know is just a response to our vibration/emotion/feelings.

"Your immediate outside physical world and your experience in that world is all, but a manifestational representation of what's going on in your mind."

So, if you think that right now you are capable of only getting Rs.10/hour for your work then think again, who decides that you should make Rs.10?? It's you who decides! It's an amount that you have mentally set for yourself because it corresponds and fits comfortably with the self-worth that you have set for yourself.

So, do you understand what this means?? Increase your self-worth to increase your net worth!!

Nevertheless, you would say, but I don't have enough experience, I don't have what it takes, I am not talented, not creative, others who are doing well, have had some advantage with them, or they were just lucky!! I am slightly on the heavier side, or I have bad skin, and funny teeth, I always take bad pictures, I am not camera friendly, but all around me it's all so bad, the economy is bad, I can't get a good paying job near my home, every person I like doesn't like me back, I don't have enough money. They are out of my league! There is something wrong with me! What if because of my small and barely noticeable idiosyncrasy people laugh at me behind my back?

Have I covered them all, or is anything left?

These are all thoughts that lower your self-worth; this is you saying I am not worthy!

"I want all the things that I want and I know that I am good enough to deserve them, but because I have bad skin I can't go to the moon!!

Yep, that sounded rather absurd!

So, first of all, stop comparing yourself to others, they have their own life experience that they have created by putting their thoughts, feelings, and beliefs out in the universe.

You are the one who decides your self-worth; your belief about your worthiness is all that matters. Everything that we have till now used to evaluate our self-worth loses its power when faced with belief. Intelligence, looks, creativity, lineage, everything comes in a distant second place to belief.

Achievers achieve because they believed they would, and so heavens and earth were moved.

So, what are you worth?

Reveal the POWER within you!

This is the first time in the history of mankind that we are openly talking about the power of the universe, rather than fearing it or worshiping it, we are actively developing our skills to efficiently communicate with it.

Through our imagination, thoughts, and emotions and by the power of our 'Will' we are now able to shape and reshape and eventually perfect our own experience in this life.

'Nothing is impossible and 'Nothing is out of reaching matter who you are and no matter where you are or how hopeless things seem for you... Just know this, it will get better, and even better, you have the power and the talent and the capability to make it better! You don't have to wait; you don't have to suffer anymore. The unlimited and awesome power of the universe is at your disposal, and when you learn to use this resource, you become unlimited and all-powerful!

So, go ahead and create!

"What has happened up to this point in your life doesn't matter.

If it's something good, appreciate it, love it, and rejoice with it. If it's something you regret, just gently acknowledge that it was also your creation,

and very gently let it go. Don't blame yourself or others. It was no one's fault. Now, standing in your 'NOW' Moment, you are free, and you are the all-powerful creator, who is fully aware of his/her power over the universe. Just take this moment to bask in your glory. You are unstoppable and invincible. You are all powerful; you are the universe itself, that's all that matters.

"We are LOAers! We are aware of our power! We are supermen and superwomen!! The 'Now' moment is our Point of power, whatever we give our positive vibrations to, the universe will create, nothing is impossible for us. This is how the human race invented air travel, discovered electricity, and changed the world. This is how we create our world, by letting go of the past and creating our future NOW!!"

Know your accountability, and duty!!

YOUR ATTENTION PLEASE, No one is coming to save you. This life of yours is 100% your responsibility.

We are all responsible for our own life and life experience. Also, there is that fact that we have only one life and if till now things have been happy and good, then good for you but if there is something you wish that was different or some regret or something that you have wanted for a long time and hasn't come yet... something stuck, then... GET UP, WAKE UP, and do something about it!!

With the knowledge of the law of attraction, we now are aware of the fact that our thoughts and emotion shape our life. Regarding the areas of our life which are troubling to us, things are going to head in one of three directions, either It's going to get worse it's going to get better, or you are going to spend another year stuck in the rut that you are in right now, and you will hate yourself for it, and then it's going to get worse.

So, what can you do to move? Well, you have to keep in mind a few things.

- First, there is no shortage, and there is no competition. There is more than enough of abundance, money, love, and happiness to go around, so just throw the "Shortage out the window and start expecting whatever it is you want."

- You are the most worthy person you know, you deserve everything you want, no one is out of your league, no job is above you, and you deserve to be happy. Go to the mirror look yourself in the eye and say the following affirmation 10 times.

"I am willing to release the need to be unworthy. I am worthy of the best things in life, and I lovingly accept it."

- No one else can get in your way, you will get whatever you put in your 'Point of attraction' i.e., you will get whatever you want, what others are doing doesn't matter; they don't have any say in your experience. If right now they are bothering you or controlling you annoying you or running away from you, just know that they are just responding to your vibration of lack or limitation, and as soon as you switch over to the vibration of abundance. They are all going to cooperate in creating your awesome experience.

So, you see... the white knight in the shining armor you are waiting for isn't coming, look in the mirror, you are the white knight, so just get on that horse and ride to victory!!

Revealed Why does GOD allow so much suffering??

AWESOME QUESTION:

I was intrigued by a post u pinned that said: Life is easy. How would you explain this just out of interest to the person with chronic ailments; with those that struggle to put food on the table every day and keep a roof over their family's head; when unemployment is just around the corner, or worse those that live permanently in refugee camps that are in hot fly-blown places like Ethiopia with no chance of ever escaping them. Upon arrival there the mother has a very sick baby suckling on her breasts that don't produce milk because she is severely undernourished to how can you then say life is so easy? I'm just curious to know.

AWESOME ANSWER:

Here is how the universe works; everyone on this planet is the creator of their own experience. If you have a brief idea of the Law of attraction, then you would know that whatever we feel, the universe multiplies. So good feelings bring more good feelings thoughts and things, and bad feelings attract more bad feelings thoughts and circumstances. Now let's first talk about the disease or chronic ailments. Disease or any ailments of the mind or body, are attracted

by a person, you grow cancer, it's your screwed up vibration, whatever is happening to the body is just a physical manifestation of what's going on in the mind, so if the mind is sick with stress and tension, and negativity, the person will fall sick, and in cases where a person holds on to this chronic negativity for a long time, he or she develops a chronic illness. The universe doesn't care about right or wrong or good or bad, it just listens to your feelings and emotions and gives you more of that, so if a person is consumed and obsessed with stress or worry or tension and feels like that his whole life is being consumed by the circumstances, he will attract a chronic illness like cancer or AIDS.

Now let's talk about people in misery, the malnourished, and war-affected people, who start their life in misery and end their life in misery. When a child is born, he doesn't know what's going on around him, he doesn't care if his parents don't have money to buy milk to feed him, all he knows is that he wants milk and so he/she cries. Now let's apply the LOA here, people in such adverse conditions are mostly stuck in such adverse conditions, because they don't know otherwise, all their life all they have seen is misery and death and poverty, and so, the primitive lizard brain kicks in for survival, and their life starts and ends for just survival. People in such places, in fact, all over the world are just reacting to their external circumstances, so the universe is giving them more of those circumstances, it's a vicious circle. And all they have to do to get out is to not acknowledge what is wrong and just dream. Now you will point out that how can a person in hellish conditions dream?? Yes, they can! Dreaming about a better life doesn't cost a thing, and if there is a slim chance that just vibrating/feeling the right feelings can get a person out of the hell he is in, then why not take it?

All these people, the ones with their ailments and the ones in hellish conditions. All of them are responsible for their own experience in their life; the universe is at everyone's disposal. All they have to do is ask for the things they want, rather than beat the drum of all they don't want! and so, I state again, LIFE is F%$KING easy!!

Yes there will be misery, there will be things that will bother you, but it is you who has to choose whether to be bothered by them or not, The Pain is real, but the suffering is optional, and it always, eases up things to know that the universe is on your side, no matter who you are no matter where you are. The pain won't last long once you stop the suffering. It will fade away and the things that will make you happy will come into your experience if it's food then it will be food if it's good health then ga great a cure for your ailment.

'By changing your mind, you change everything.

The moment you stop being bothered by all that is wrong with your life, the moment you stop paying attention to all the misery, the moment you stop counting the things that are out of place, your vibration will start rising. At first, you will 'feel Nothing', A Void, which is better than feeling 'bad', Then as your vibration rises, you will start to feel happier and at ease, and then, before you know it, doors will start opening up where there were only walls. You will see a solution to your situation.

How to transform anger, pain, and worry into Love!!

How to let go of anger, pain, and worry! The simple process with LOA is that you decide what you want, then you "feel" like you already possess what you want, and the universe then picks up on your 'feelings' and delivers to your whit precision what you want.

But what if you can't feel it?? What if you can't feel anything? Or when it comes to having the feeling of having the evidence from the past, stand up and stare at you right in the face??

Sometimes, you go in for a quantum leap, you don't release the past, and focus on your desire so hard, that the universe delivers to you your desire, but because you haven't let go of the anger and the pain, you see your desire turn rotten in front of you.

You manifest things but you have difficulty holding on to it...

You lose the money you manifested, your soulmate now seems like the devil, and the dream job you manifested, is starting to feel like your last few jobs, which you hated.

All this happens, when we, just jump into the visualizing, daydreaming manifesting mode, without facing our demons.

So...is your dream relationship turning rotten for no real reason? The person you were supposed to feel love, for now, you seem to hate?? It might be that you are still holding on to the pain or suffering caused by this person or from previous failed relationships. You know that it's all now ancient history, and this pain seems illogical. However, nonetheless, it is all too real and you are angry inside, but you know that anger is a negative feeling, so you try your best to suppress it, distract yourself... and forget about it... and slowly you feel a state where you can't feel anything at all.

That was one example... wanting more?

So why is it, that the people who shoot up to fame and fortune fast or win the jackpot and rake in a lot of money fast, can't seem to hold on to it? (There is scientific research analyzing this phenomenon). The faster the fame and money come the faster they crash and burn.

It's all happening because we have learned to practice the Law of attraction, but we are still holding on to the Limiting beliefs, the anger, the pain and we haven't fully grasped the concept of letting go.

SO, WHAT DO I DO??

You work through the anger, the pain, and the suffering. After learning so much about LOA, you do realize that you are the one who attracted all that suffering pain, and bad experiences to yourself. Though like any normal human being you find it easier to point out to a recipient external to you, whom you can hold responsible foyourou pain, who you can be angry with, and whom you can accuse for all that is wrong in your life.

I suggest you do that! Of course, not to that person's face but you can always vent out at them in your thoughts...here is what you do.

Take out some time and find a quiet place where you can be alone, now pick up a person or a situation or god (if you are angry with god), you hold responsible for your misery... now they are there to listen to you, and you are there to vent out you... can scream at them, shout at them, call them names, reason with them, you can take a pillow, imagine it's them, and Go all Lucha libre on it for all I care. The goal here is to get angry and vent out, don't leave anything, you can beat that pillow to an inch of its life, but instead of suppressing your anger for all this time... try to take it all out.

Some people think being angry is a bad emotion, it is, but it is better than self-hate, depression, and frustration. When you get angry, you are actually in a higher vibration.

After you are done, you will feel lighter, and you will be able to breathe better. Repeat this exercise 3 times max (for one recipient).

With your anger out of the way, you can now look at the universe rationally, if it's a relationship you want to be healed, then you have to admit to yourself that, you just yelled and beat the shit out of the other person, so now the score is settled, you have a clean slate, and so does they and they will behave exactly as you ask the universe for them to behave with you.

So, if you can just work through your pain, you will finally find the peace you are looking for, all the uncertainty will dissolve, and you will be a powerful creator.

So go... try it...

Learn to love yourself

I learned it the hard way, but the most, important relationship in your life is with yourself. It's not with your family; it's not with your siblings, not even your lover! It's you! The most important person for you should be you.

Yes, I am telling you to be selfish, being selfish ain't a bad thing it will be the best thing that you can do for yourself. You can be selfish to a point where your actions don't cause pain to another person, but till that point, I think you are OK.

So, when I say, that you should love yourself, and put yourself before anyone else in your life, I am just reasserting the very basics of the Universes law: i.e.

"ONLY THING THAT MATTERS IS WHAT 'YOU' WANT, THE UNIVERSE LISTENS TO IT AND RESPONDS TO IT, EVERY TIME! EVERYTHING ELSE IS JUST NOISE"!

I have had my fair share of relationships, and in each one of them, I gave my best, I valued them, I loved them with all my heart and I always gave them the best of me, but when I needed to be held, when I needed love, No one was around. At first, it didn't make any sense, I thought, maybe I did something wrong, but this happened again, and in the next relationship, and the next, and then I came to the conclusion that it's not what you do in a relationship, but where you are vibrational is what matters.

It doesn't matter, how well I behave, how much love I give, it doesn't even matter how many times I travel to the moon and beyond to cater to their whims, or how many nice gestures I do for them, all of this will be in vain if I don't love myself.

"They won't love me if I don't love myself."

"They won't be there for me if I am not there for myself"

"No one is going to listen to what you want, except for the universe"

By not loving myself, I am actively blocking all the love that I can have from others, the love that I know I deserve, but am not ready to receive, because I don't think I am lovable.

I can be a pessimist if I want, but if I love and value myself, if I think that I am desirable and I see the amazing wonder that I am, the universe will respond to it, and everyone I meet will fall in love with me.

You must have known people whom everyone wants to know, everyone falls in love with (hint) these are the people who are happily in love with themselves.

You must also have encountered amazing people in every possible way, but for some reason, don't have the relationships they deserve... (hint) low self-worth, no self-love, sometimes self-hate.

You have people; no one likes (hint) self-hate!!

Now you will say, but there are so many things I need to improve about myself, I have those some extra pounds, extra baggage, extra pimples, extra emotional problems, extra daddy issues, extra mommy issues, blah blah blah

Who doesn't??? There is no perfect person in the world, get hold of your role model and ask him/her, what they want to improve about themselves, and you will get a list.

So, if you are waiting, once I deal with my current issue, then I'll be lovable again, I hate to break your bubble, but that day is never going to come.

Love yourself now, find what's good in you, and be thankful for it, appreciate it, love it, love you, and then from that place of love, set your goals of improvement.

Remember, the universe is always working for you, but you can't address the question of "What is it that you want??" From a place of Low self-worth.

No one is going to see your worth if you don't see it yourself.

So, where to start? How to start?

Well, I say:

- Make a list of 10 things that you like/love about yourself; these can be physical characteristics, qualities, achievements, talents, and anything you can think of. Take a pen and paper, and make this list, be descriptive. Appreciate all your qualities.

- Read this list every day and add at least 1 new point every day.

Doing this going to help you on many levels, it will raise your self-worth and confidence from an LOA's point of view. It will make you more attractive to yourself and others around you.

You deserved to be loved and treated like royalty, but you have to start with yourself. Treat yourself gently and with love.

Let go of worry with logic!

As creators of our world, we all know that the universe is "24x7x365x till the end of time " listening to our emotions and responding to them by bringing us matching thoughts, emotions, and circumstances. So, we know that positive emotions will pave our way to an amazing future and negative emotions will take us far into the depths of sadness and misery.

Still, most of us 'worry', we worry over small things and big things alike, it's like an automatic response to a situation that doesn't agree with us in any way. Worrying about a situation somehow makes us feel that we care, but if you just take a moment to think about it. Worrying doesn't do any good; all it does is give the universe a signal to create more worry-inducing circumstances and thoughts.

So, if you think that you are being worried about a situation because you care about it, is justified, just don't! You are making it worse! You are mixing your negative vibrations into a situation that already is negative.

People will say, but I can't stop worrying about my loved ones, my son or daughter, or my friend! It shows that I care!

Well, it's nice to care, but worrying and adding your negative vibration to theirs is the way to go, all you are doing is making them miserable and messing up your vibration.

I am not saying that you should abandon them, you should be concerned, and the right way to lift them would be to find a place of high vibration, and then pull them up, one step at a time. Bombard them with positivity, trust the universe, derive happiness from the fact that the universe will take care of your loved one, and feel the happiness you will feel when they come to you and tell you that it is all well and good now.

So, what do you do when you face a problem??

You follow this flowchart!

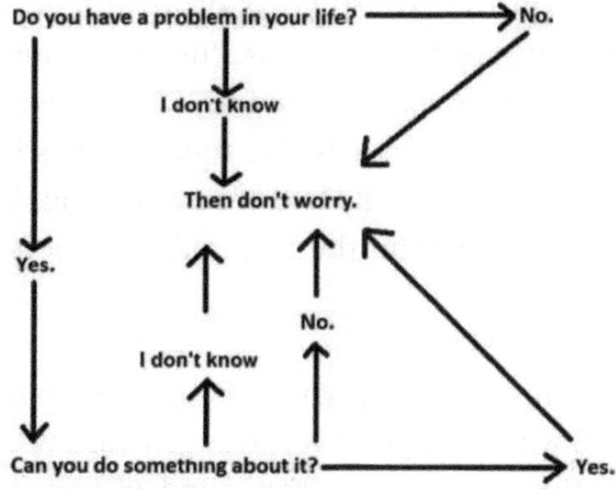

Let go of worry with Logic...

You know that whatever the situation, there is no place in your life for worry. Because even if things seem to be not in your hand, worrying about them will only make the situation worst.

But then, being a LOAer, there is no situation that's out of your hand, now is there??

Your successful start to anything goes here

A year from now you will wish you had started today.
-Karen lamb

All of us have that sudden spark of inspiration now and then, the inspiration to pursue our wildest dreams and desires, but a few 'breaking bad binges' later we are back to our 'stagnant' selves, I mean, what happened, where did the inspiration go??

Well, contrary to the popular belief, being 'unconditionally happy' is one of the harder things to achieve in life, It's easier to say, 'feel good but for a person, who has spent the last 30 years of his life developing the belief of 'things bring happiness', 'unconditional happiness is a little hard to achieve, and as LOAers we know that unconditional happiness is the foundation stone for any successful manifestation. Here are a few things that you can do when the next time the inspiration to better your life hits you.

GET UP!! AND...

1. Clean up!! Clean up your room, your apartment, your house, and wherever you live, arrange your DVD collection, mop the floors, put away the laundry, and do whatever needs to be done, sometimes clearing up your living space makes you feel good about your living arrangement and yourself. A clean room will uplift your vibrations.

2. Take care of all your chores, or things that you have been procrastinating upon, and that can be done by just giving a little bit of your time, if you have to make a call, then call! if you have to pay the bills, then pay your bills. Make a list of all the things that you need to do and have been avoiding because you are too lazy, and do them today, check tasks off the list as they are accomplished, it can be small things, but it will free your subconscious mind to focus on your desire. Also, the sense of accomplishment this activity provides feels great.

3. Start a new exercise regime, whether it's Pilates, weights, cardio, yoga, anything will do, just be sure to do it properly. I am not saying being out of shape is a bad thing, but it feels good to see yourself in the mirror and have a fabulous figure staring back at you. It raises your vibration. Also, working out causes the brain to release endorphins (The love hormone), gives you a happy high, and raises your vibration.

4. Meditate, increase your concentration and meditate on what you want. Figure out what exactly you 'want' and the answer is always a feeling. For example, you may be hung up on a particular person for a long time, you want that 'person' but in reality, what you want is a loving relationship', just make sure it's not about feeding your ego. Talk to yourself, connect with yourself. Be clear on what you want with your life, to not give off mixed vibrations.

5. Make a list of your desires; know that all of them are going to be yours. Because you are THE EXTENSION OF SOURCE!! YOU ARE THE UNIVERSE PHYSICAL MANIFESTATION. YOU ARE AWESOME.

NOW GRIN UNCONTROLLABLY!!!

That's how you start!!

You can make good things happen more quickly by thinking about them more...

"Want" and "desire" consist of wanting "to focus attention, or give thought toward a subject, while at the same time experiencing positive emotion. When you give your attention to a subject and you feel only positive emotion about it as you do so, it will come very quickly into your experience."

It's never too late to start the change!

"Many of us feel as if we are running out of time. Many of us, when first inherit this knowledge of the universe and LOA, start regretting all the things that have gone wrong in the past, things we could have done differently.

Well, it's ok, you can start now, you don't have to live with the beliefs that you have created till now, and if that belief is in some way not serving your wellbeing, then it's better to let go of that belief and create a new one.

Beliefs are just 'thoughts' that we think over and over again, we think them to be true because they are our 'practiced thoughts'. So, the good news here is that you can always create a new belief, by practicing a new and better thought.

So just think about an area of your life that is not working out for you and, find out what is the limiting belief you are holding regarding it. Think the opposite thought of your belief. And slowly and gently try to play with the possibility of this new thought being true.

So, when is the right time to start a change?? I say 'Now!', and after 5 minutes if you ask me the same question, I'll say 'Now', a month later ' NOW'. It's never too late, as the universe keeps aside all your desires and manifestations safe for you until you give up the resistance and start to believe and invite the manifestations in."

One of the biggest diseases of the mind is overthinking. Especially too much thinking about others, when you are constantly thinking and speculating about all that is wrong or might go wrong, or the reasons why something you want isn't going to come, you are flooding your mind with negatives, and the universe doing what it does best is also flooding your mind with similar negative possibilities. All these thoughts have weight! Not to mention all these thoughts are creating something, the first creation is a "bad feeling/panic

attacks/anxiety/restlessness" and if you don't stop there then, what follows are bad things happening to you.

Thinking too much is like eating too much, the heaviness makes it Impossible to remain light and flexible.

So, take a breather!!

It's OK! Whatever may be the circumstance, it's OK! Once you stop acknowledging the things that are causing you pain, once you stop being bothered by the things bothering you, you will notice that the things causing you pain, will start to fade away, and eventually, the things you love and enjoy will start to replace them, The trick is to hold yourself in the place of 'calmness' long enough so that happiness can step in and believe me, happiness isn't far away.

So how do clear you your mind? I'll say you Meditate.

In addition, there is a tip.

YOUR DAY-TO-DAY EXPERIENCE IS JUST A PHYSICAL MANIFESTATION OF WHAT'S GOING ON IN YOUR MIND!

Whatever you believe about yourself on the inside is what you will manifest on the outside.

It can't get simpler than this!! If you can just acknowledge this one simple fact, then you can change your whole perspective of life and the living of life.

Bad days can be transformed into good days in just a few moments, and problems could be resolved in moments. The universe always works instantly, the moment you set an intention, its manifestation starts. The universe starts shaping your circumstances accordingly so that your intention can be met.

So right now, at this moment...

What is your intention? How are you feeling?

Are you creating something wonderful? (And creating something amazing)

Or

Are you stressing over something negative? (And complicating the situation even more)

Are you appreciating yourself? (And getting younger and happier and healthier by the moment)

Or

Are you holding on to some limiting belief about yourself?? (And Gaining weight, loosing hair, losing money and love and respect)

"It's better to trust your emotions than over-think a decision."

In other words: Listen to your intuition. Instead of overthinking your choices, let your emotions guide you toward what is right and what is wrong. This will result in a more satisfying life. So, what is going on in your mind today??

The Dilemma!!

- Decision-making tool. Do I walk away or do I try harder??

Ahh, the big question that's haunting everyone since the dawn of time is, 'should I try harder for that one thing that I have always wanted, or do I walk away and save myself further pain and misery??'.

The answer to this is really simple, but first, we have to address both the 'WALKING AWAY' and TRYING HARDER' states of the dilemma.

People feel like 'WALKING AWAY' on a desire because it's not been fulfilled for a long time, but it's been on your mind every waking moment of your existence, and with every passing moment you feel like, that things are not getting better, or you are nowhere near to achieving your desire. You have persisted for so long because all you wanted was this one thing to be done and then you thought you will be happy. However right now at this moment when you think about that "DESIRE" that's not coming to you, it causes pain, sometimes you have endured that pain for so long that you become numb to it, and it only hurts when Things get worst, for others, it's like that nagging song that you don't like but it's stuck in your head and it plays 24 x 7. So yes, the prospect of "WALKING AWAY" does give you the feeling of momentary relief, but as soon as you start thinking about a world without your "desire" you start to feel empty and the process starts over again, it's one of the reasons why "walking away" is so hard.

Now, walking away doesn't always mean giving up or losing. You can always walk away with the intent of finding something better. Be it your current desire or a desire for a better alternative, the universe will cater to everything.

Now let's talk about "TRYING HARDER"! I mean WTF!! Can't you just say "TRYING", why in the world did you have to attach a degree of "HARDER" with it?? Now you will say, "if it was not hard to achieve my desire then I would have it already and I wouldn't be reading your book."

Well, it just seems hard, because of all the evidence of failure that our stupid little mind has accumulated for so long. Don't pay attention to the mind!! Our mind thinks that it knows everything there is to know. Plus, it fails to acknowledge any new thing without evidence, and even after getting evidence, it wants further evidence, thus the feeling of uncertainty that a young man feels when the girl of his dreams, whom he thinks is out of his league, responds positively to his advances.

I say that the "TRYING" isn't "HARD", it's not even "TRYING" once you get the hang of #LOA. We all know that we live in a vibrational world and that the universe is listening to our every thought and responding to our every emotion.

This limiting Evidence that you always bump into, is your creation only, it's a result of your Doubt and fear-filled vibration (screwed up vibration). Just acknowledge the fact that it's all in the past, it does not affect you. Just acknowledge it and LET GO.

Now whatever may be your "desire", if you focus on its achievement completely and feel the way you would feel when you have your desire, the universe will respond to your vibration and deliver you your desire, and that almost instantly. But what happens is that when we do try to feel like we would when we will have our desire, the above-mentioned, evidence pops up, and we are being creatures of habit feel bad, and decide that these obstacles are real. They are not real; they are just external manifestations of our mental limitations. Remove them, and you will have your desire the next day.

So, in the end, it's a choice, but this choice between 'walking away" or "persevering" should not be made from a place of 'LOSS', i.e., Don't pick up the "walk away" option because the other option is impossible for you, or you are tired or fed up because then it's hardly a choice. Same way doesn't pick up the "trying" option because for some reason you think that you can't walk away now, or you are out of time or late.

Know that both options are possible and feasible and most importantly EASY, and which one ever you choose, at the end of it you will be happy.

The universe is on your side and is responding to your emotions and getting you exactly what you are asking for. So, ask for the things you want, if it's something you have wanted for a long time then, let go of the fact that it's not possible to achieve because it's easy to achieve once you let go of the evidence.

How to receive mammoth mammon (money)

If it's money you want to hold on to, then you have to acknowledge the fact that the universe is capable of providing you with unlimited financial abundance, and you are doing well where you are and you will always do well financially.

Well, by acknowledging that it's not BIG. When it comes to the universe Rs.10 is the same as Rs.100,000 is the same as Rs.10,000,000. It's you who makes the difference and we do that because often we associate the action or work with money. So, earning Rs.10 is a small thing, and earning Rs.1 million is a BIG thing because the amount of action or work associated with making a million would be huge.

Most of us don't even know if we are capable of that much action or not. But here is the catch, the universe only responds to your vibration, and so if you can just acknowledge the simplicity of this conundrum,

i.e., if the amount of money you receive is just equal to the vibration you are offering, then you are good to go. The key is to replace the word "Earning" with "Receiving" and the word "effort/action" with "Vibrational offering"

Vibrational offering = Amount you receive.

Secret of Success

So, what if you are not where you planned to be???, so what if the things that you have wanted for so long that you think you deserve are still not there?? It doesn't matter, because you can't judge yourself on the fact that there is something that you still haven't achieved...because once you have your current desires, you will have more desires, and then once you have them, you will have some more, you will never be in that state where you will have it all, coz desires grow as we move forward in life and if for some reason you do reach a place where you don't desire anything else... Then I think you have stopped growing.

There is always something you will want. Acknowledge the fact and stop focusing on the absence of things that have not yet manifested.

The things you have always wanted are actively moving closer to you, acknowledge this fact also because it's true, the universe is tirelessly and constantly working on a way to get your desire to you. Yes, it's taking time, but it's taking time because you are constantly delaying it by paying attention to its absence, but when you will stop that, and yes, you will eventually stop, the universe will smack you, right in your face with your manifestation. All you will do then is try to wipe that grin off your face. Or don't, grins are good.

So, LOA is all about the process... it's a journey, you can't declare failure just because the road leading to your destination is a long one. Just be calm,

acknowledge that you are moving towards your destination, and let the universe take you for a ride.

If things haven't gone your way lately, don't be hard on yourself, often people who are new to the Law of attraction beat themselves up over all that has gone wrong in the past, and all that is wrong in the present. That is not going to help, it's just going to create more pressure on you and signal the universe to create more of what is 'wrong'. Just breathe and be gentle with yourself. Treat yourself like you would treat a 5-year-old child. I mean would you beat up a 5-year-old for his screw-ups or would you talk to him lovingly and nurture him, preparing him for future success?

Story of Life -The Carrot, Egg, and Coffee.

(You will never look at a cup of coffee the same way again!).

A young woman went to her mother and told her about her life and how things were so hard for her. She did not know how she was going to make it and wanted to give up. She was tired of fighting and struggling. It seemed as if one problem was solved, and a new one arose.

Her mother took her to the kitchen. She filled three pots with water and placed each on a high fire. Soon the pots came to boil. In the first she placed carrots, in the second she placed eggs, and in the last, she placed ground coffee beans. She let them sit and boil, without saying a word.

In about twenty minutes she turned off the burners. She fished the carrots out and placed them in a bowl. She pulled the eggs out and placed them in a bowl. Then she ladled the coffee out and placed it in a bowl.

Turning to her daughter, she asked, "tell me what you see. “Carrots, eggs, and coffee," she replied.

Her mother brought her closer and asked her to feel the carrots. She did and noted that they were soft.

The mother then asked the daughter to take an egg and break it. After pulling off the shell, she observed the hardboiled egg.

Finally, the mother asked the daughter to sip the coffee. The daughter smiled as she tasted its rich aroma.

The daughter then asked, "What does it mean, mother?" Her mother explained that each of these objects had faced the same adversity - boiling water.

And each had reacted differently.

The carrot went in strong, hard, and unrelenting. However, after being subjected to boiling water, it softened and became weak.

The egg had been fragile. Its thin outer shell had protected its liquid interior, but after sitting through the boiling water, its inside became hardened.

The ground coffee beans were unique, however. After they were in the boiling water, they changed the water.

"Which are you?" she asked her daughter. "When adversity knocks on your door, how do you respond? Are you a carrot, an egg, or a coffee bean?"

Think of this: Which am I? Am I the carrot that seems strong, but with pain and adversity do I wilt and become soft and lose my strength?

Am I the egg that starts with a malleable heart, but changes with the heat? Did I have a fluid spirit, but after a death, a breakup, a financial hardship, or some other trial, became hardened and stiff? Does my shell look the same, but on the inside am I bitter and tough with a stiff spirit and hardened heart?

Or am I liking the coffee bean? The bean changes the hot water, the very circumstance that brings the pain. When the water gets hot, it releases fragrance and flavor. If you are like the bean, when things are at their worst, you get better and change the situation around you.

When the hour is the darkest and trials are their greatest, do you elevate yourself to another level? How do you handle adversity? Are you a carrot, an egg, or a coffee bean?

May you have enough happiness to make you sweet, enough trials to make you strong, enough sorrow to keep you human, and enough hope to make you happy.

The happiest of people don’t necessarily have the best of everything; they just make the most of everything that comes along their way.

The brightest future will always be based on a forgotten past; you can't go forward in life until you let go of your past failures and heartaches!

9 798888 151082

Printed by Libri Plureos GmbH in Hamburg, Germany